To Chapinouche, Ronron, Paul Pigeon, Loupiot and Mirò

Groundwood Books / House of Anansi Press
720 Bathurst Street, Suite 500, Toronto, Ontario M5S 2R4
Distributed in the USA by Publishers Group West
1700 Fourth Street, Berkeley, CA 94710

We acknowledge for their financial support of our publishing program the Canada Council for the Arts, the Government of Canada through the Book Publishing Industry Development Program (BPIDP) and the Ontario Arts Council.

ONTARIO ARTS COUNCIL
CONSEIL DES ARTS DE L'ONTARIO

Library and Archives Canada Cataloguing in Publication
Gay, Marie-Louise
Caramba / Marie-Louise Gay.
ISBN 0-88899-667-5
1. Cats–Juvenile fiction. I. Title.
PS8563.A868C37 2005   jC813'.54   C2004-907329-X

The illustrations are in watercolor, pencil and pastel.

Printed and bound in China

CARAMBA

written and illustrated by
MARiE-LouisE GaY

A GROUNDWOOD BOOK   HOUSE OF ANANSI PRESS   TORONTO   BERKELEY

aramba looked like any other cat. He had soft fur and a long, stripy tail.
He ate fish. He purred. He went for long walks.
But Caramba was different from other cats. He couldn't fly.

It worried him a lot.

"Every cat in the world can fly," he said to Portia, his best friend, "except me."

"I'm different, too," said Portia. "I'm pink and fat. I have a curly tail…"

"You're a pig," cried Caramba. "All pigs are pink and fat."

"…and I can't fly, either," said Portia.

"Pigs don't fly. Cats do," sighed Caramba. "Everyone knows that."

It was true.
Soon after they learned to walk, young cats would begin to fly.
They would leap off the cliffs and soar over the ocean.

Caramba watched them swoop and glide and skim the waves.

"That looks like fun," said Portia. "Don't you even want to try?"

"No," said Caramba.

But secretly Caramba did try.
He jumped off a small rock…
and fell flat on his face.
"What are you doing, Caramba?" asked Portia.
"I'm looking for caterpillars," mumbled Caramba, his mouth full of grass.
"For my caterpillar collection."

Then Caramba leaped off a chair…
and landed in his grandpa's lap.
"Ay, Caramba!" cried his grandfather. "What are you doing?"
"I'm admiring your slippers," muttered Caramba. "They're very nice."

Caramba decided to try on a windy day.
He ran as fast as he could and flapped his arms.
"What are you doing up there, Caramba?" asked Portia.

"Just hanging around," said Caramba, "waiting for my socks to dry."
Finally, Caramba gave up.
"That's it!" he told Portia. "I'll never fly!"

"*What?* You can't fly?" said Bijou.

Caramba looked up. His heart sank.

His cousins, Bijou and Bug, were hovering just above his head, purring loudly.

"That's ridiculous," said Bug. "Every cat knows how to fly."

"Caramba can do other things," said Portia. "He collects caterpillars, he tells stories, he cooks cheese omelets…"

"But he can't fly!" laughed Bug.

"Caramba, what is wrong with you?"

Caramba didn't answer.

What could he say? That he was afraid to fly? That flying made him dizzy?
That he had tried over and over again and failed every time?

The cats flew away, giggling and weaving between the clouds.
"Let's do something else," said Portia. "Let's go for a ride in the rowboat."
"I don't want to do anything else," said Caramba. "I want to be alone."

Caramba walked slowly down to the pier.

"What *is* wrong with me?" he thought. "Why am I different?"

He wondered how it would feel to fly –

to float like a cloud, to be light as a feather, to be free as a bird,

to be like all the other cats.

It probably felt wonderful.

Then, with a furry whirring noise, Bijou landed on the pier.
"I have an idea, Caramba," said Bijou. "We'll give you a flying lesson."
"What if you drop me?" said Caramba. "What if…"

"Don't be such a scaredy-cat," said Bug. "Cats are meant to fly."
Bijou and Bug each grabbed one of Caramba's paws.

Up they went. The wind whistled through their fur.
Birds swooped beneath them.
Caramba opened his eyes. He was amazed. He could see forever.

He could see forests and rivers, red roofs on tiny houses,
the patchwork squares of fields.
It was stupendous. It was scary.

Now the ocean glistened, moving like a giant animal stretching out beneath them.
"Are you ready?" asked Bijou.
Caramba's throat was dry. "No!" he whispered.

But they didn't hear him. They let him go.
"Fly, Caramba!" cried Bijou. "Flap your arms! Whirl your tail!"
But Caramba fell like a stone into the dark water.

Bubbles rose around him.
Seaweed tickled his paws.
Caramba opened his eyes. Schools of fish were staring at him.

Crabs scuttled over the white sand.
Sea urchins and starfish basked in the blue light.
Caramba's fur waved softly in the water. He was floating!

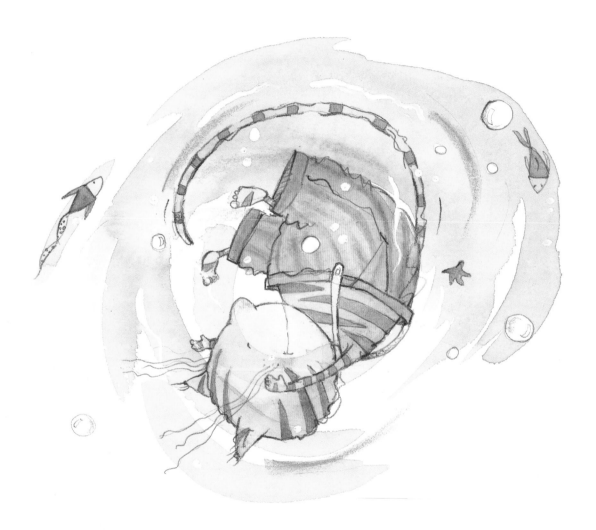

Caramba flapped his arms… and glided through the water.
Caramba whirled his tail… and soared through the seaweed.
He somersaulted and swooped.
He was light as a feather. Free as a bird.
It was like flying!

Up above, Portia, Bug and Bijou were very worried.
"Caramba!" they called. "Car-r-r-ramba!"
Suddenly Caramba popped out of the water. "I'm here!" he cried.

His cousins stared in amazement as he swam toward the rowboat.
"What are you doing?" cried Bijou "Cats can't swim! Everyone knows that!"
"Well, I can," said Caramba.

"How was it?" asked Portia.

"Wonderful!" said Caramba, drying his ears. "You should try it."

"I just might," said Portia. "Who knows? Maybe pigs can swim, too."